ILLUSION OR REALITY?

For a moment, sitting in a cab on Seventh Avenue and Twenty-third Street, Jerry Fletcher was in Hell—not literally, of course.

This was worse than the real thing. The flash of a white strobe light transported Jerry to a terrible place where shadowy figures strapped his arms and head down. Jerry shut his eyes. Maybe he could make it all go away. Please God. If only the light would stop.

Jerry cocked his head to listen to the sound of conspiratorial whispers. He could not make out the words. He watched helplessly as the hallucinogenic figures pumped the contents of a syringe into his immobilized arm.

His perspective got woozy as he heard approaching footsteps. His eyes darted back and forth trying to spot whoever or whatever was nearing. It was close by.

Without warning, Jerry's eyes widened with unanticipated agony. The room and the figures within may have been an illusion but Jerry's scream was the real thing. . . .

CONSPIRACY THEORY

BY

J. H. MARKS

BASED UPON THE MOTION PICTURE WRITTEN BY BRIAN HELGELAND

A SIGNET BOOK

SIGNET
Published by the Penguin Group
Penguin Putnam Inc., 375 Hudson Street,
New York, New York 10014, U.S.A.
Penguin Books Ltd, 27 Wrights Lane,
London W8 5TZ, England
Penguin Books Australia Ltd, Ringwood,
Victoria, Australia
Penguin Books Canada Ltd, 10 Alcorn Avenue,
Toronto, Ontario, Canada M4V 3B2
Penguin Books (N.Z.) Ltd, 182–190 Wairau Road,
Auckland 10, New Zealand

Penguin Books Ltd, Registered Offices:
Harmondsworth, Middlesex, England

First published by Signet, an imprint of Dutton Signet,
a member of Penguin Putnam Inc.

First Printing, July, 1997
10 9 8 7 6 5 4 3 2 1

🟤 REGISTERED TRADEMARK—MARCA REGISTRADA

Printed in the United States of America

Chapter 1

The yellow cab sped along Second Avenue as though it were being chased. Dodging in and out of traffic, it took advantage of every opportunity to race a little faster or to pass cars blocking its way. Lights turned from yellow to red and the driver tore through intersections, leaving cursing drivers in the cross streets. By nature, New York City cab drivers were a belligerent species but the man behind the wheel of this particular car gave a whole new meaning to the term "defensive driving."

Alarmingly blue eyes darted between the cab's windshield and rearview and door mirrors. The eyes were not afraid but businesslike and studied the surrounding landscape for potential adversaries. Was the American sedan three cars back driven by salesmen from Long Island or somebody more threatening? What was the deal with the Mercedes that pulled away from the curb only moments after he drove by? Who was the suit in the crosswalk and why was he glaring after the cab in that menacing fashion? Why did he raise his hand in that unusual way? Was he reporting the cab's location to someone over a hidden microphone? The blue-eyed man hit the gas and surged forward at even higher speeds.

But when the cab driver checked out the rearview

mirror and took a closer look, he realized that his "antagonist" was just a businessman who was swearing and giving him the finger. The driver grabbed a cigar from his box of Supremas and laughed to himself. It was true he had driven a little too close to the pedestrian. But there was nothing to be worried about. He was a highly skilled veteran—experienced in evasive tactics, well versed in the rules of combat, and a master of the survival techniques that were necessary to maneuver in a hostile environment.

The suit in the crosswalk was cursing at the wrong guy. There were plenty of people in Manhattan who posed a threat to ordinary citizens. The cab driver didn't think he was one of them. On the contrary, he was always on the lookout for those who did.

The driver turned west on 42nd Street and chose not to waste any more time thinking about the infuriated pedestrian. It was unlikely he had taken down the cab's license number and besides, the driver had his own problems to worry about.

He wasn't sure but it seemed to him that he was hearing a voice. A faint and tinny sound that swore and encouraged him to do terrible things to himself. It was barely audible over the competing sound of the traffic. The cab driver was in the middle of a long shift and didn't like the idea that he might be imagining things. There was only one thing to do. A simple solution. The driver lit his cigar and flipped off his radio. The voice stopped. His dispatcher had been yelling at him to acknowledge a pickup on 38th Street, but the driver didn't want to answer and wasn't going to bother to explain. He had his reasons. At the end of the day he would apologize and say something vague about competitors monitoring the airwaves.

way that should have conveyed the image of a strong, handsome man who knew his place in the world.

Strangely enough, that wasn't the impression most people had of him. What wasn't obviously apparent about Jerry Fletcher in a glance soon became so. For all of his good looks and natural charisma there was something troubling about the way he carried himself. It wasn't that he appeared to be dangerous per se, but Jerry Fletcher's passions often got carried away and crossed a border into a more overheated, hyperactive condition.

Jerry was just a little too fervent about subjects that interested him and he talked too rapidly and too much about them. When he smiled or laughed, Jerry Fletcher was an appealing and terrific guy. But when he didn't, when Jerry was lost in one of his obsessions, when his mind worked overtime, he was a potentially unstable and quirky figure.

In all likelihood, Jerry Fletcher had been born a good person. But it was also clear that he had wrestled with personal demons in the past and was still in the process of trying to elude them. In his loopily manic approach to life, Jerry Fletcher was too engaging to be intimidating, but it was also abundantly clear that he had more than a few screws loose.

The cab swerved suddenly across the lanes of traffic and pulled to a stop in front of a typically massive Manhattan apartment house. Obscenities flew. Brakes screeched. And not a few hand gestures were offered in the general direction of the offending vehicle. Jerry took it all in stride as the normal interplay of the mad and courageous who dared venture down New York's suicide alleys.

Instead of returning the offensive salutations, how-

What annoyed him most about the foul-mouthed dispatcher was that the name he had been shouting over the radio wasn't the driver's real name. Instead the dispatcher used the same epithet the enraged man in the crosswalk had shouted after him. The truth was that the driver's actual name had nothing to do with the less glamorous sections of a person's anatomy. His real name was Jerry Fletcher.

Jerry was not a run-of-the-mill New York City cabby. For starters he spoke English as a first language and actually knew how to get to Brooklyn without getting lost. More than anything, however, Jerry wasn't born to hack, even though he was good at it. It was clear just to look at him that there was too much going on in his head to be satisfied with hauling fares. In some ways he seemed like a guy who was driving a cab while taking time out from the real work of his life.

What that vocation might be could be anybody's guess, however. To glance at Jerry Fletcher the first thing a person would notice were the vivid clarity of his blue eyes. To simply call them blue, however, didn't quite do justice to their singularity. Over the years women he had long forgotten tried, and failed, to describe them. Dictionaries had been plundered and Jerry's eyes had been variously called aquamarine, azure, indigo, turquoise, navy, royal, and even sapphire. Often the waters of different oceans were invoked—including the Caribbean, Mediterranean, Pacific, and at the end of a relationship, even the Arctic—but none fully captured his distinctive vitality.

If you could break away from Jerry's mesmerizing gaze a person might next notice the attractively constructed design of his face—jaw, nose, cheeks, mouth—everything working together agreeably in a ever, Jerry's eyes flashed to his rearview mirror and scanned the traffic that sped by him. The coast was clear. Anybody bold enough to tail him would have been caught red-handed. Jerry was pleased. With no one pursuing him, he was free to pick up the fare that his dispatcher had been yelling about. Jerry looked at the empty doorway of the apartment building and tooted his horn.

A moment later the apartment door opened. An attractive thirty-something woman and a man a few years her senior stepped out and lost themselves in a passionate good night kiss. If most cabbies would have turned away—either out of respect for the couple's privacy or because they resented the man's good fortune—Jerry kept his gaze firmly upon them and smiled as the couple lingered in each other's arms. Jerry himself was madly in love with a wonderful woman and he was always pleased to see others find happiness as well.

As the man made his way to the cab, Jerry noticed the young woman watching her lover depart. The man stepped into the cab, shut the door, and gave Jerry his marching orders. "Luxembourg Towers on Seventh." Jerry nodded and rolled the car out into traffic. Both men kept their eyes on the young woman as she stepped back into her apartment house and shut the door. The man sighed deeply.

Jerry took this as the opening salvo of a conversation and dove right in. "The sound of love."

His customer's mind was elsewhere—no doubt back in his lover's arms—and he wasn't sure if he had heard right. "Excuse me?"

Jerry imitated the man's heavy sigh and explained, "That's love." The man in the backseat had a more cynical approach to life than Jerry and disagreed with the cabby's romantic sensibility.

"Love? Love's just a pretty way of saying, 'I want to sleep with you.' Love is bullshit."

Despite the fact that Jerry had been hacking a New York cab for quite some time, he still possessed a certain idealism—at least about some things. Not one to edit his thoughts, Jerry felt compelled to defend the good name of romance. "I live on tips, so don't be offended, but you're a liar. I saw you kiss. Admit it, this is the street where love lives."

The cynical lover turned around in his seat and glanced back at his girlfriend's home as the cab hurtled down Third Avenue. The cab driver had a point, as much as the passenger did not want to admit it. The man had been away from the woman he loved for no more than forty seconds, all of seven blocks, but already he missed her. Still, it was not a New Yorker's way to easily admit to such sentiment. He faced forward as Jerry turned the cab a little too quickly onto Twenty-third Street and headed west. The passenger listened while Jerry pronounced, "Love gives you wings. It makes you fly. I don't even call it love. I call it Geronimo."

"Geronimo?" The passenger had heard love described in many ways, but never like this.

Jerry explained, "Geronimo. When you're really in love, you'll jump. Off the top of the Empire State Building. Screaming Geronimo the whole way down."

Even to a man flush from the warmth of his lover's bed, the notion of taking a dive from the roof of a skyscraper seemed pretty impractical. "But you'll die. You'll squash yourself. What's the point?"

Jerry accelerated through a yellow light and scat-